Greta
Groundhog

Greta Groundhog

Dave and Pat Sargent

Illustrated by
Blaine Sapaugh

Ozark Publishing, Inc.
P.O. Box 228
Prairie Grove, AR

Library of Congress Cataloging-in-Publication Data
Sargent, Dave, 1941-
    Greta Groundhog / Dave and Pat Sargent ; illus-
trated by Blaine Sapaugh.
        p.   cm. -- (Animal pride series ; 20)
    Summary: A young groundhog learns skills
for surviving in the wild. Includes facts about the
physical characteristics, hehavior, habitat, and
predators of the groundhog. Includes facts about
the physical characteristics, behavior, habitat, and
predators of the Groundhog.
    ISBN 1-56763-041-3, -- ISBN 1-56763-040-5
(alk. paper)
    1. Woodchuck--Juvenile fiction.   [1.
Woodchucks--Fiction,]   I. Sargent, Pat, 1936-
II. Sapaugh, Blaine, ill, III. Title. IV. Series:
PZ10.3.S243Gr 1996
[Fic]--dc20   96-1489
                                      CIP
                                      AC

Ozark Publishing, Inc.
P.O. Box 228
Prairie Grove, AR 72753

Inspired by

February second, Groundhog Day.

Dedicated to

my daughter Daina. I will love
you forever and always.

Foreword

A young groundhog has to leave home and is faced with many surprises.

Contents

Greta
Groundhog

One

Greta Groundhog

"Greta!" Mama Groundhog called. "It's time to come in now."

Greta stopped playing and glanced toward the burrow. She didn't want to go inside. She wasn't through playing. Finally, she turned to her friend and said, "I have to go in now, Robbie. Can you come back tomorrow?"

"Sure," Robbie answered, with a grin. "See ya, Greta."

Robbie headed south toward his den, taking the well-traveled trail that ran between his den and Greta's den.

Greta's three brothers were waiting for her just inside the entrance to the burrow. They were ready to tease her like they did every evening.

As she entered the den, Willie the Bully chanted, "Greta loves Robbie! Greta loves Robbie!" Then, running circles around Greta, he asked, "Don't you, Greta—huh—don't you?"

Completely ignoring Willie, Greta looked neither right nor left. She walked straight ahead until she reached her mama's side.

Mama Groundhog smiled at Greta and said, "You're learning,

Greta. If you continue to ignore your brothers when they tease you, they will soon stop. They tease you because they love to see you get mad. When they realize they can't get to you anymore, they will probably stop teasing you. Like my mama used to tell me about my brothers, 'Ignore them and they'll go away.'"

"I'm trying, Mama," Greta whispered, "but they can be such a bother."

"I know honey, but they'll grow out of it," Mama Groundhog said. "You'd better get ready for bed now."

"Okay, Mama. Good night."

As Greta started toward her corner of the burrow, Mama Groundhog whispered, "I love you, Greta. You're a good girl."

"I love you, too, Mama," Greta said, with her sweetest smile.

When she curled up in her bed that night, she felt very happy and content. She felt loved and wanted. Even her brothers wanted her. She was certain of that. Without her, they would have no one to tease.

Right in the very best part of her dream, Willie the Bully and Greta's two other brothers, Wally and Walt, pounced on her bed and began jumping up and down, yelling, "Come on, Greta, wake up! It's time for breakfast. Hurry! Mama is taking us to Farmer John's alfalfa field this morning!"

The boys had startled Greta, and her heart was racing. Before the first three words had cleared Willie's mouth, she sat straight up on her haunches. When she saw that it was only her brothers, she dropped to the floor with a sigh of relief. She didn't like waking up so fast. It made her head pound!

Greta didn't call out for her mama, and she didn't yell at her brothers. She simply looked each of them straight in the eye and, with a calm voice, said, "Please leave my room. I have to get dressed."

Willie the Bully and Wally and Walt had no intentions of leaving Greta's room. That is, not at first. But the little gleam that she got when she meant business was creeping into her big, round black eyes, and they saw it.

Wally and Walt tugged at Willie the Bully's arm and said,

"Ah, come on, Willie. Let's go outside and wait for her. She's no fun, anyway."

When Greta finished grooming herself, she went in search of her mama.

Mama Groundhog was waiting just inside the back exit to the burrow. She took the young groundhogs to the lush field of alfalfa, where they ate their fill.

Mama Groundhog had been busy for the past two weeks, preparing four dens. One for each of her children. It was the twenty-eighth day of June and time for the young ones to leave her burrow.

That evening when Greta and her brothers went inside, Mama Groundhog called, "Greta, Willie, Wally, Walt! Come here! I want to talk to you."

When the four young groundhogs gathered around their mama, she said, "I have prepared a den for each of you, and tomorrow I will take you to live there."

Greta didn't know whether to feel happy or sad. Oh, no! She would have to leave her mama!

But most of all, she would have to leave Robbie. "Who will I play with?" she wondered.

Her next thought was of her three brothers, Willie, Wally, and Walt. The same brothers who had teased and tormented her since she was three weeks old. She knew without a doubt that she would really miss them—especially Willie the Bully.

Greta thought about what her mama had once said about Willie being a natural-born leader. "I guess Willie could be a leader if he would stop being a bully. Bullies can't be leaders. No one looks up to a bully," she reasoned.

Early the next morning, Greta opened her eyes and noticed the empty room. She got up and walked through the den. It was empty. There was no Mama—no Willie, no Wally, no Walt. There was no noise. Not a sound could be heard. Nothing.

Two

Greta's New Home

Greta rushed to the front entrance of the burrow and sat up on her haunches, looking and listening for any sign of danger. And then, about five hundred yards away, her sharp eyes detected movement.

"It's Mama and Willie!" she exclaimed, wondering where they were going—forgetting what had been said the night before.

She waited at the entrance of the burrow. It wasn't long before she saw her mama coming back. She ran to meet her, asking, "Where did you take Willie, Mama? And where is Wally? And where is Walt?"

Mama Groundhog said, "I have taken your brothers to their own first den. Greta. I told all of you last night, remember?"

"Now I remember," Greta said.

Knowing that it was her time to go, she went to her chamber and gathered up all her favorite things.

Mama Groundhog was at the front entrance, waiting for Greta. She asked, "Do you have all your things?"

Greta looked up and saw a tear in her mama's eye. She said, "You're going to miss me, too, aren't you, Mama?"

"Of course, I will," Mama Groundhog answered, as they went out the door and down the path.

Greta suddenly realized that she knew the path well. She and Robbie always played in the clearing that was just ahead and to the right. She smiled a secret smile, happy that she was going to be living in a familiar place.

Mama Groundhog glanced over and saw the smile on Greta's face. She was pleased that Greta was happy. It was important to her.

Greta looked to her right and saw a freshly dug den. She hurried over to it. She stopped at the entrance and asked, "Is this my new home, Mama? Is it?"

Mama Groundhog said, "Yes, at least until midsummer, then you may want to find a bigger home for yourself. You will want children of your own one day, and then you will need more room."

Greta stopped just inside the entrance to the burrow. She saw that it would keep her safe and dry. She was proud and happy to have her own home. It meant that she was almost grown.

She hugged her mama and said, "Thank you for my new home, Mama."

Mama Groundhog said, "You're a big girl now, Greta, so you must make your own way. I'll be close by if you should need me." And with that, Mama Groundhog left Greta's new burrow and headed back to her own den. Before she disappeared into the woods, she turned and waved.

"Bye, Mama. I love you," Greta called in a trembling voice. She looked hard but could no longer see her mama. Mama Groundhog was gone. And suddenly, she felt very alone.

"I'll be all right," she thought. "I'm a big girl now." She raised her head, put a brave smile on her face, and walked out into the sunshine.

About fifteen minutes later, someone yelled, "Hi, Greta!"

Greta whirled and jumped about a foot into the air! She had thought that she was completely alone. Then she saw him. It was Robbie—her best friend.

"Hi, Robbie!" she called as she ran to meet him. She was happy to see a familiar face.

All the while they were busy playing, Greta's keen eyes were noting several places she could find food and water. Yes, she was going to love her new home.

They ran around some thick blackberry bushes right into two big brown eyes, a long black nose, and long, sharp,white teeth!

Ole Barney the Bear Killer growled. He was on the trail of Chrissy Cottontail, and the two young groundhogs had startled him. They had given him a big surprise.

"When a cottontail rabbit runs into a blackberry thicket, groundhogs are not supposed to run out!" Barney thought as he stopped growling and sat down.

"Who are you?" Greta asked, with her heart pounding.

"I'm Barney the Bear Killer," Barney answered, with his chest thrown out.

"Bear Killer?" Greta asked with big round eyes, "Does that

mean you've killed a bear?"

"Of course, it does," Robbie said, in an excited voice. "That's what you call someone who has killed a bear—Bear Killer!"

Greta said, "I've never known anyone who has killed a bear! Are you mean?"

"Shucks, I'm not mean," Barney answered. "I had to kill an ole grizzly because he was killing Farmer John's baby calves—and he was trying to kill me, too!"

"Oh, my!" Greta whispered excitedly.

And Barney, with his chest stuck out, added, "I help take care

of all the animals here on Farmer
John's place. I keep them in line,
if you know what I mean. It's my
job."

"Boy, you sure do have an
important job, Barney, and you
sure are brave," Greta said, as she
looked up at him with admiration
in her eyes.

Barney blushed and said, "Groundhogs have an important job, too. That's what Farmer John says. Well, guess I'd better be going. I'm supposed to help move some cows today, and I can't be late."

Greta watched as Barney trotted off through the woods.

She asked, "I wonder what Barney the Bear Killer meant when he said, 'groundhogs have an important job, too'?"

Robbie shook his head and said, "I don't know, Greta. Maybe we'll find out one day."

Three

Ole Baldy

A few weeks later, Greta yawned and opened her eyes. She felt different somehow.

She crawled out of bed and looked around her den. She had never noticed how small it was. She needed a bigger home.

After breakfast, without giving it much thought, she gathered up her favorite things and headed out in search of a new home.

Two days later she was wishing that she had located a new home before giving up the old one. She didn't like living in the open. It was scary, and it was very dangerous!

At that exact moment, Baldy, a large bald eagle circling high above Greta, looked down.

When he spotted Greta, he

thought, "Now there's a nice juicy groundhog. That young ground-hog will make a nice-sized dinner for me. I love rats, and I love rab-bits, and I love squirrels; but most of all, I love tender young ground-hogs! Yum, yum, yum!"

Baldy circled and picked up speed, then went into a nose dive. He shot down toward Greta like a speeding arrow. His eyes zeroed in on her, and his mouth watered.

Down below, Greta sensed danger. She quickly looked all around, but saw nothing unusual.

Then she heard it. It was a swooshing sound—the sound a jet makes when it slices the wind. It was a dive bomber coming straight for her!

She ran for the nearest berry thicket as fast as her short, fat legs would carry her. And just as she dived under it, Baldy landed on the ground with a thump—on the exact spot where she had been standing only seconds before.

Craning his long powerful neck, Baldy searched the ground for Greta. Then he spotted her under the berry thicket.

Trembling, and knowing that she was in terrible danger, Greta wished desperately for her mama.

Just when Baldy stuck his long, wicked-looking beak under the berry thicket to grab Greta, something wonderful happened.

Robbie had been following Greta, trying to find her. And

now, seeing the terrible danger
she was in, he ran up behind the
huge bald eagle and with his
strong teeth grabbed Baldy by the
leg and bit down as hard as he
could!

Baldy let out a loud screech!
He drew his long, skinny neck
from under the berry thicket and

glared at Robbie with his black beady eyes.

Robbie dived under the thicket and, grabbing Greta by the hand, yelled, "Run, Greta! Let's run as fast as we can!"

They ran and ran, and just when they felt they could not take another step, they came to a hole in the ground. They tried to stop. They teetered and tottered, then fell down and down—into total darkness.

Greta screamed! Robbie yelled! Then silence.

They tumbled, slid, rolled head over heels, and finally settled. "Where are we?" Greta asked in a whisper.

"I don't know," Robbie answered. "Are you okay, Greta?"

"I'm okay," she said.

"Me, too. Come on, let's look around," Robbie said, as he started off.

Greta heard excitement in his voice. She was excited, too! She loved to explore caves and dens and holes in the ground.

Suddenly, without warning, Robbie disappeared from sight. She was about to call out when she heard, "Wow! Look at this!"

Following the sound of his voice, she turned to her right and saw a large, empty room.

She held her breath, then exclaimed, "Oh my! If only I had a home like this!"

Robbie said, "Maybe no one lives here. Maybe it's deserted."

They explored every chamber. Greta felt at home. She knew that she could be happy in this new-found burrow. She hoped no one was living in it.

After waiting and watching the entrance to the burrow for three days and not seeing a soul, Greta moved in. She was certain now that it had been abandoned.

Farmer John and Barney had finished milking the cows and putting out the hay. They had broken the ice that covered the ponds so that each cow could get a drink, and now, they were on their way to the house to have breakfast.

Amber, April, and Ashley ran to meet their daddy. Farmer John reached down and picked up Ashley and said, "Morning, ladies. Do you remember what today is?"

They nodded, then asked, "Do you think we'll see a groundhog today, Daddy?"

"If we don't take too long with breakfast," he answered.

After they finished eating, they set off—Farmer John, the three little girls, and Barney.

Farmer John and Barney knew that a young groundhog had

moved into the empty fox's den, and that's where they headed.

When they neared Greta's burrow, they hid behind a berry thicket and waited.

Down in the burrow, Greta woke up. She groomed herself, then hurried to the entrance of her burrow. She felt special today.

When she walked outside, she looked all around, then said, "It's going to rain, or snow, or sleet, or something! Just look at those big, white clouds! Oh, boy! I hope it snows! I love to play in the snow!"

She hurried to the clearing. Robbie was coming down the lane. She was glad to see him.

Sixteen eyes peeking out from behind the berry thicket saw Greta leave her den and run down the lane.

There came a whispered voice that said, "Yes, siree, would you look at that? We can always count on groundhogs. Looks like we'll have an early spring!"

Groundhog Facts

A woodchuck, also called a groundhog, is a small animal that belongs to the squirrel family. Groundhogs live in Canada and in the eastern and midwestern United States.

Legend says that a person can tell when spring will come by watching what a groundhog does on Groundhog Day, February 2. On February 2, the groundhog pops out to check the weather. If it is cloudy, it means an early spring. A sunny day means six more weeks of cold weather. This belief traces back to an old European tradition in which the hedgehog and badger do the weather forecasting on the same date.

The groundhog that lives in North America is about two feet long, including its bushy tail, and has a broad, flat head. Its coarse fur is grayish-brown on the upper parts of its body and yellowish-orange on the under parts.

Woodchucks dig complex burrows or dens that contain several chambers. There are usually three exits: front, back, and a drop hole. The drop hole opens onto a straight shaft that goes down two or more feet. The woodchuck may sit next to the drop hole, observing an approaching intruder until the last moment, when it drops out of sight into the safety of its burrow.

When a woodchuck goes to look for food, it first sits up on its haunches at the entrance to its burrow. Though a woodchuck appears complacent when it sits up, it is scanning its environment for signs of danger. Its hearing is acute, and its eyes can detect movement seven hundred yards away. Woodchucks eat alfalfa, clover, and fragrant grasses.

In winter, the woodchuck hibernates from December to

March in a special den that has only one entrance. The nest chamber is plugged in November, and its occupant sleeps undisturbed until early spring. It eats large amounts of food in the fall before hibernating. The extra food changes to fat in their bodies, and the woodchucks live on this fat during their winter sleep.

In April or May, female woodchucks give birth to four or five young. Before June has passed, the mother leads each one away to its own first den, which she has prepared in advance. By midsummer, a young woodchuck will go to a new field where it digs a burrow for itself.

The woodchuck will grow fat on many kinds of pasturage. Its long front teeth never stop growing, so they must be ground down constantly. Some farmers consider woodchucks to be pests because they frequently destroy crops.